Mysteries beyond the Gate

& other peculiar short stories

OTHER BOOKS BY MATT RAWLINS

The Question
The Namer
The Container
Rediscovering Reverence

LEADERSHIP BOOKS
The Green Bench
A dialogue about Change

The Green Bench II
Ongoing dialogue about communication

Emails from Hell

The Lottery
How a question can change a life

Mysteries beyond the Gate

& other peculiar short stories

By Matt Rawlins

Amuzement Publications

Cover by Delvyn Hunter

Dedication

To Aimee, Micah, Matt, Mark, and Katherine.
Thank you for allowing me into your world.
I love you.

Table of Contents

The Gate

Chapter 1

I awoke from the dream in a cold sweat. Haunting images hung at the edge of my mind. I shook my head back and forth to send the haunting images back into my subconscious mind. I decided to go for a walk. I hoped a steady walk might help my world get back in order.

With the movement of my body arose questions for my mind. 'What if there was light? How could I dream about something that didn't exist?' The family secret, oral traditions of my great grandfather, came back to my mind. There was a place where light was everywhere. It was said that sight was what we were made for. Images described and passed on to each generation.

Yet, darkness was all I had ever known. The darkness closed in for the first time in my life and I felt its weight upon me. I usually enjoyed its privacy and the intimacy it offered. Yet for the first time, the dreams provoked me in ways I never thought possible. The dream's images begged my company and with my waking will, I allowed them a place in my thoughts, taking courage that darkness was only a choice away. I closed my eyes and the gate slowly grew in my mind until I could see it clearly, it was a wall of light, like a fire only pure white. No smoke arose from it yet the flames, like waves or..., I could not find the words to describe them as they were like nothing I knew, rushed towards me. I stared trying to understand what was going on around the gate, but I couldn't make the images out.

I opened my eyes and the world of darkness grabbed me. Ahh, darkness that covered, that hid, that protected you. A new thought arose, protected me, from what? In an instant I knew, I had to try and find the gate. I had to see if there was light. If there was a gate or anything like it where people could live and understand the world around them because of the light.

I heard the familiar sounds of my friends close by. As I said good-bye and explained where I was going, they tried to stop me.

They reminded me of the folklore we had all accepted as reality, light would kill you with its heat.

My oldest friend picked up the charge, "You don't know what you're doing. You are searching for a dream, and dreams are not real. Give it up."

"I agree it seems far fetched, but think about it. Every group or person I have ever talked with or heard about, knew about light.

I have never heard of any group that did not have some reference point or discussion about it. How can that be so if there is no such thing as light? I don't understand."

"Light is just a creation of our mind. It is something that is created by those who are not content with what they have and where they are at."

"That is my point, maybe we are not meant to live in this darkness. We have settled into it and accepted it, but were we made to live in it? All I know is that when I see my dreams of light, in a terrifying way, it feels normal. How could that be for someone who has grown up in the dark?"

"A man feels wet when he falls into water, because man is not a water animal: a fish would not feel wet. I guess in a nutshell, if there was no light in the universe and therefore no creatures with eyes, we should never know it was dark. Dark would be without meaning."

"But darkness has great meaning to us, we love it and yet hate it. We hide in it and secretly discuss light and what it would be like and then quickly settle into our darkness as it is more comfortable for us. I will not do that again without at least searching for the gate of light that I see in my dreams."

My friend gathered himself for one last shot at me, "OK, what if you find the light? What happens then? Ever wonder what the light will reveal about you? Ever wonder what darkness hides us from? What if darkness was given as a gift to hide us from the agony of the light? What if, when you see yourself, it is terrifying beyond anything you know? You will be stuck with that knowledge the rest of your life. Are you willing to live with that? At least here we are comfortable and can create what we are and what things look like. In the light you will lose that gift. What if reality has a life of its own, and what if you are not welcome?"

My friends words cut to the core of my being. I broke out into goose bumps mingled with a cold sweat. I had never heard anyone say so clearly what we all intuitively understood and feared.

My girl friend walked over and wrapped her arms around me and gave me an intimate kiss. "I am going to miss you. You know we make pretty good light between us!" she said seductively.

Thankfully she broke the terror of my friends words, and resisting the sudden strong urge to stay with her, I turned and started walking, "I will miss you too," I said as I walked off.

I did not know where I was going, but trusted that I would know somehow as I went. I had not been walking for more then an hour before I saw a faint light. I stopped dead in my tracks and just stared, thinking my mind was playing games with me. I so wanted to find the light that I thought my mind had created it on its own. I closed my eyes and turned in a circle to disorientate myself and tried to find the light again. I turned back in the direction that I thought I had seen it before and saw it again. It was as if my choice to find it, had given me freedom to see it. Why had I never seen it before? Surely I had walked this way many times? Darkness grew stronger around me. Never before had I felt its weight pushing against me. I headed toward the light, afraid that if I waited any longer it might fade and I would have nothing.

Chapter 2

Somehow the distance passed without problems and I could slowly make out what was ahead. There were people. My great grandfathers images were not too far off. There where large tents set up that spread out in the light. I walked down into a little valley and along it for a while and finally up and over the last knoll.

Light was all around me. No maybe that wasn't true. I couldn't see any light just the results of the light. I raised my hands to cover my eyes as the brightness of it caught me off guard. A fleeting thought reminded me of my friends last comment. Maybe he was right. I put it aside and peered out through my hands at all that was going on around me. I turned to look back into the darkness out of which I had come and could only see a hundred feet down into the valley. The ground was a reddish brown dirt that blended into the darkness quickly. I turned to face the light hoping I could see and realized my eyes had adjusted to the light. A smile broke out on my face as I realized I was made for the light. How else could my eyes work so well at adjusting to it?

I saw a group of people near by and went over to explore. Excitement building at the thought of seeing this light and through it, seeing myself and the world around me.

A thread of silver light was reflecting off one of the tents, like a cord on fire, came out and pierced the darkness, finally landing a good distance from the tents. A small group was huddled around the place where it landed. It seemed they were interested in the light, but only from a distance. One man in the center, stood on a stand and held up a box. At first I couldn't understand him. As I got closer I could hear his pitch, "Get your light, right here. Packaged in these light weight, easy to carry, air tight boxes. See for yourself, I found a way to catch the light and packaged it for you myself, and for only a very small fee. Trust me folks, you won't find anything like it anywhere else. You can avoid the helter skelter of all these people and get right at what you came here for. You wanted light, here it is. You can even head back out in the darkness and take the light with you. This box can be yours. Step up right now, own your own light. One at a time, there is plenty for everyone. Don't be shy, you don't have to get any closer to the light, it can be yours..."

A voice called out from someone who had just bought one, "My light is gone, what happened."

The man on the box answered at once, "Oh, yes, I forgot to tell you. As soon as I shut the box, you must not open it for one day or you will let it out and it will be gone. Bring the box back to me and I will put it in and then be careful not to open it for one day so that the light becomes accustomed to your box."

Something didn't sound right but I dared not question him. Who was I to question him, after all I just came out of darkness. Marveling at the wonder of it I looked closer. For who would not want to have their own personal light. I heard someone mumble about how they had to buy one to take it back to prove to their friends they had been right in coming. I thought of the look of my friends face when I would show them the box. I could prove I was right. I pushed closer to get a better picture. Seeing the small beam coming off the tent high up, and landing out here, the man would hold his box at just the right angle so any who looked, could see the box was full of light. I was so tempted to get one of these little boxes of wonder but decided it would not be enough. I didn't want a little box of light I wanted to live, bath, drink and feel the light. I could never do that with a little box of it. Besides I had to look for the gate.

I stepped back and looked around. There was so much more to see.

Chapter 3

I walked closer to the tented area. I was close enough now so that light was every-where. I noticed green shoots growing thick from the ground. I guess I should say I no-ticed a soft substance under my feet first. As I looked to see what I had stepped in, I noticed the green shoots were so thick it was like a carpet. They grew on their own in the light and it made it like walking on clouds. I stared down at my feet for the first time and noticed how red and dirty they looked. Filthy toe nails, scarred and callused feet. I then starred at my legs and then quickly up at my waist, and then my hands. My hands were covered in dirt and what must have been a life's worth of stains, blood, and grime, filthy blackened nails in-cluded. I looked around at those walking past me and the weight of what I looked like hit me. I am filthy.

My friends words came back again to me harder then ever. Light exposed me to oth-ers. In complete shame I stood before those all around me and realized I had never cleaned myself. Light cared not a wit for me. It would not guard me. It would not protect me. It would only expose me. I thought of running back to the darkness. What horrors lie ahead of me with such a foe. Was there such a thing as a pain worse then death? Was this the death the folklore spoke of.

How could I fight such an enemy except with darkness? Everyone could see everything I did. I would have no place to hide. Just as I was about to turn back, the grass caught my attention again. Such a soft beautiful welcome it gave. I realized new things could grow in the light that could never survive in the darkness. As I let this new idea settle in, it gave me hope and I continued towards the tents. A few people stared at me and I quickly moved on. There were some coming in from the dark, like me, out at the edge but I noticed most of those closer to the light were cleaned up. I realized the light left you no choice. You either cleaned yourself up or went back into the darkness. More determined then ever, I pressed on.

I tried to stop a young couple passing by, "Excuse me, I am new here and I...." They gave me a quick glance and moved on, hoping I would leave them alone. Finally one young women motioned to a tent and told me of a bath tent close by and then she swiftly moved on. I quickly found the tent and went in.

They had small enclosed stalls and I was led into one by a kind old caretaker. He mentioned, "Stay as long as you want, and you may need to refill the tub several times before you can scrub yourself clean. There is soap there on the edge, clippers and a scrubber, everything you should need to clean up."

I mumbled, "Thank you very much" and went inside. I stood for a moment, staring at the steaming bath, enclosed in the safety of my little area. Safe from staring eyes, with a way to clean myself. I slid into the water and went to work. I watched in amazement as within minutes the water turned into a red clay color. I realized the wisdom of the old caretaker and redrew my water to start the process over after the initial dipping.

After the clay was scrubbed off, while washing my arm, I noticed little hairs on my forearms. I just stared. The water was exposing new parts of me. What a wonder water was. Why had I cared so little for water? Then it hit me. It wasn't the water, it was the light. Light revealed everything for what it was. It did not make anything different, it just exposed it. It did not attack as I first thought. It was not a foe ready to defeat me. I was my own foe if I could not bear who or what I was. It was me that could not stand the light. If I could not stand up to the exposure of what light revealed, then I would have to blame the light to stay sane. For to not blame the light would be to accept its harsh reality and that, was the terror my friend spoke of. I leaned back into the tub of hot water and soaked. I had spent my whole life afraid of the exposure of myself. Tears flowed as I realized that I was responsible for what I had become.

I washed and scrubbed, I clipped and chipped, I sanded and soaked and scrubbed some more. Finally, I felt clean and got out. The old caretaker brought some new clothes and I dressed myself. Aware for the first time what it meant to be clean. A wasted and useless thought if there were no light. Now a desire and pleasure fulfilled in the light.

I ventured back out into the park with a new sense of confidence that I could fit in with the others. To my satisfaction I realized no one stared at me or even gave me a second look. I was considered one of them.

As I went back along the edge of the tents, I turned and saw a strange sight. There were people that looked disgusting. I could not believe anyone could be so filthy. Then it hit me, they were people coming in out of the dark. Aware of my recent cleansing I quickly found myself withdrawing and wanting to not be seen anywhere near them. Then I stopped dead in my tracks and thought about what I was feeling. Moments before, I was one of them. I knew how they felt, yet I didn't want to accept that I did. There was a battle going on inside me. Should I acknowledge that I was like them, only clean? Or pretend, like so many others around me, that these filthy people were different from me, that somehow the cleaning process had removed that part of me that was like them and now I was better.

It seemed a question that dealt with how I would live in the light. Yet, I couldn't understand quite how.

I decided that they needed help and I could offer it. I walked out to welcome them to the park. They seemed surprised at my welcome and asked what they should do. I pointed to the cleaning tent and explained the process to them. They quickly went towards the tent. I spent the next hours finding as many as I could see coming out of the dark and helping them find their way. It seemed the best I could do.

Chapter 4

When it seemed like no new people were coming in and a few of those I helped were waiting to help others, I turned to explore the other tents. Walking down a path between them each seemed full of different people.

Before I knew what was happening a man grabbed me by the arm and pulled me into his tent. I dared not resist. He had been here longer than I, and being a stranger and enjoying the light so much I didn't care where I went.

"I can tell you are new here," he started out.

"Yes I am," I replied.

"Good, you won't be aware of the problems going on around us and what to do, so we will help you."

"I would appreciate that very much," I responded as they seemed very willing to help a poor lost soul trying to find his way.

"First you must be aware of the different lights that are going on all around us here. You may not recognize it yet, but there are different lights all around you and you need to know that we have the best light in the park."

"I thought light was light." I stuttered not even sure how to respond.

"We have a special system set up so that the light that is mirrored in here is the purest and best light anywhere. In fact, I don't want to brag but this tent may have the only true light in the whole park. We allow new comers to join us, but we are careful about those that have been around for a while and don't believe what we believe. Come with me, we have some classes that will teach you all about who we are and why we have the best light."

I was gently pulled across the area. As I moved I noticed everything was in perfect order and everyone was dressed similarly. I had not seen those styles on anyone else, they seemed so out of place, but who was I to judge. Finally I was told to sit down with a group in the corner, deep in their tent. An older women was using a stick to point at a chart that was set up. She droned on, "We were started by a man who passed through the gate many years ago."

With that my heart skipped a beat and I said out loud, "There is a gate here? What is this gate you are talking about? Where is it?" I asked at once.

The old lady stopped her monotone dialogue and looked over at me with her long scowling face. She stared at me for a moment and then said, "He is long gone, but don't worry we have kept his words alive. Don't worry about the gate, it would be safer for you to stay here with us. We can teach you what you need to know. Remember, we have the light here," she pointed to a huge mirror set up near the roof that directed the light into the tent. "And I might add that if you leave us now, you may lose your way and you definitely won't have the proven traditions and clarity of light we have here. Do you want to walk outside this special place and be mugged and die without the this light?" She said these last words with a long pinched face.

It sounded like a warning, like a threat to keep me in the tent with them.

I thanked her for her advice but said that I had not seen enough yet and desperately wanted to learn more. As I left they tried to warn me of the others but I must confess, it fell on deaf ears as I was so interested in all that was happening. I stepped out to see some more.

Chapter 5

I walked down the walkway and continued towards what seemed to be stronger light. It is hard to explain as things were not brighter around me. It just seemed more intense, more penetrating, if that is possible. A part of me was uncomfortable in going forward. Yet, another part was awakening within me.

I rounded a corner and there was an entrance to an area like none other that I had seen. A clown stood juggling at the entrance to this amusement park. Behind him, colors and sounds were going off in every direction as it begged, it called, it captivated every sense in my body and pulled me inside. Every possible way of entertaining a person could be found in this area. I guess it shouldn't come as much of a surprise but by far, most of the people were in here. I too heeded the call and went inside.

In one corner there was a set of large screens set up with every imaginable sport showing on them. There was also free coffee for anyone who wanted it. A band played soft music. The words of the music were all about the beauty of light and how it had helped so many.

I joined in all the activities and days passed like minutes. You could go from one event to another, to another, on and on they went. Each event was perfectly timed so that there were so spare moments, no quietness, no time to reflect or question anything. I couldn't get enough. I couldn't stop.

On one ride that went high in the air, I waited my turn and jumped into the seat. I sat anticipating this new feeling that I was sure would come. The cage rose high in the air and the first time around I saw the darkness out beyond the tents. I thought of my friends and where I had come from. Questions began to rise in my mind. On the next time around I looked into the tented areas and I thought I saw, for one brief moment, a bright light. I was stirred anew with images of the gate. I had forgotten all about it.

I got off the ride and asked myself, 'Where are you?' 'What are you looking for?'

I turned and found a young women next to me, "Excuse me, have you seen a gate with light?"

She turned to me and responded, "I don't know anything about a gate with light."

I pressed a little bit, "Do you know where all the light comes from?"

She gave me a concerned look, "What does it matter where it comes from? It's just there, look what it has given us, isn't that enough?"

I thanked her for her help and began to ask around if anyone else knew where a gate was or where the source of the light came from. No one seemed to care, they were all preoccupied with being entertained. They were too busy to even think about the source of the light.

Remembering the stronger light that I thought I saw from the ride I turned to leave the area. I began to wonder whether all this entertainment was just a more subtle form of darkness.

Chapter 6

As I walked down the walkway I noticed a tent that was closed off. I arrived at the entrance where there were guards to keep people out. I walked over to one of the openings and looked inside. It was breathtaking in it's beauty. There was a rock wall on one side with a cascading waterfall that flowed into a small pool. Banquet tables were set up with food beautifully arranged and stacked high on them. I noticed they were set up for a fashion show and there were models walking around those sitting at the tables showing off the latest designs. It was pretty obvious that the guards were there to keep out anyone who was not one of them. It was automatic that no dirt of any kind would be allowed in there.

A man walked up to me and handed me a pamphlet and asked, "Would you sign this petition please?"

I turned, "I may if you will tell me who these people are? How you get inside? Where those lights they have in there come from and what the petition is for?"

"Well, my friends inside are the who's who of the park. Anyone who is anybody joins here. You have to be invited to join by someone who is already a member and you have to have money. The lights come from generators that they had build so that they could better control the lighting they wanted. With the park's source being outside their tent they wanted more control over the lighting in case something happened to the park's light. They don't like being dependent on others."

He took a breath and continued, "As for the petition, they want to build a new wall at the edge of the darkness with a new gate that would be open at certain hours. It would be much easier to control those coming in and going out."

He leaned over close to me and whispered, "Besides, wouldn't it be nice to make those coming in from the dark clean themselves up before being allowed in the park?"

Startled by the response I said, "But they don't know they are dirty until they get into the light! That's like telling someone to clean up before they clean up."

He seemed uninterested in my response so I asked a simpler question, "Why don't they just build the wall themselves? They seem to have plenty of money!"

"Well, I guess they would never go that close to the edge of the park. They rarely ever leave the safety of their own tent. They want to have nothing to do with all the dirt and filth that is out there. They want the park to do it and they would help to fund it."

A question popped into my mind, "How high would this new wall be?"

"Well that is not exactly stated but they have hinted that it would have to be high enough to keep out any intruder, so the higher for them the better."

"But that would block the light from being seen by those lost in the darkness," I declared.

He shrugged his shoulders, "There is a concern that we don't want to have too many people here as that could lead to over crowding and might strain the supplies that are available."

"I appreciate your help in answering my questions but I can't sign the petition. I think we need to help as many people as we can who are lost." With that I turned and walked away. I wanted nothing to do with that group.

Chapter 7

I continuted down the alley. The intensity of the light became stronger. The air was so thick with it you could almost cut it. I knew I had to be close to the gate. As I rounded a corner, I was literally struck by the light. I closed my eyes and almost fell back from the surprise. I slowly regained my composure and opened my eyes to find there was a group before me blocking the way. I eagerly pressed into the crowd to get a better look. Before I could catch myself, I found myself tripping over some poor soul who had fallen before me. I tried to get up and to help the guy I had tripped over. I offered my hand but all he could do was point. I looked up hesitantly at where he seemed to be pointing and there was a man standing on a small rise right before us in the light. I blinked my eyes a couple of times and looked again. Caught up in the beauty of the light, for this was the first time I had actually been in it. Standing, with bright light seeming to come from him, stood a man with arms out stretched calling all the people to come to him. The light was so bright and blinding you couldn't help but think that it was coming from him. Especially as this was the first time I had actually seen the light. I quickly forgot about the man I had fallen over and began to move toward this source of light.

As my eyes were fixed on him, all of a sudden a shadow passed behind the man. For one brief second he stood there, a man. Looking so small and foolish. He was standing so that the bright light was shining out of an opening and if he stood just right he knew that those who were coming up from the darkness would think that it was him giving off the light and would look to him. Someone walking behind him had blocked the light when they went by the opening, I looked back at the man I had tripped over and he was still bowed down, so caught up in his initial view that he didn't bother to look any farther. I gathered myself up and moved around the crowd and those kneeling before the man. I was too close now to give up or settle for an imitation.

Chapter 8

I continued staring at the gate and moved closer. There was one more group between me and the gate so I walked over to them. I figured anyone as close as they were had to have something special going for them.

There were broken up into small clusters huddled around instruments. I joined one group and watched them for a while as they worked with their instrument.

Soon I asked, "What's that for?"

One of them turned towards me with his finger over his lips, "Shhhh, we are testing for any sound in the light, we want to know if the light makes any noise and the instrument there," he pointed at it, "we built to test for any sounds that might be associated with the light."

"And what about the other groups," I whispered.

He began pointing and whispered back, "Well, that group's testing the heat of the light, and that group's testing for fluctuations, and that group's studying the people who come to the gate,"

I grew excited and interrupted him, "You spend your time studying the light! You must know a lot about it and really love it."

He tilted his head down to look at me over his glasses, "Yes, we do study the light, but I don't understand what love has to do with it. We are only interested in what we can objectively validate with our testing. We have no choice but to be this close because this is the only way that we can get accurate readings on it. We have just reached unanimous agreement that this is light, whether it is a wave or particle is still highly arguable. We are pretty sure it is not the only light and we are hoping, to soon be able to understand its makeup so that we can duplicate it ourselves and use it more effectively than it is now."

"Why don't you just step into it. That would be a great way to understand it."

"Oh, that would be too subjective and against our ethics. We must fully understand it before we are comfortable with it. Besides, right now we are only concerned with studying it for the betterment of mankind. That is our primary concern. Analyzing it is more important than any single benefit it might give to an individual." With that he turned back to his small group to get the latest reading on his instrument.

I looked at these groups of men and wondered at them. They were so close, they could reach out and touch the light and yet, they hid behind this supposed objectivity to

protect themselves from any personal respon-
sibility to it. I marveled at them, the mask of
darkness crept up to the very edge of light, and
yet would not accept its reality and walk in it.

Chapter 9

I stood and just stared at the gate. Questions running through my head.

An old man appeared next to me and asked if I needed any help.

"Was the bath I took and all this necessary?" I asked, pointing to the tents I came through.

The old man hesitated, "No, some of those from the darkness sense the light is here and walk directly to it and then into the gate. The experiences out there are usually things that happen after you make entrance, or they can be tests and preparations for people to see if they really want to make it here. Many times those that have made entrance, come back out and begin to express their love for what the light has done or to reach those coming into the darkness. But after they come back through the gate to stay, those that pick up the work after them may miss the point and soon the gate is not as important as the work itself is and its effectiveness dies. A culture or identity usually forms and people narrow down the purpose of the light to just their expression or understanding of it. I do know that people get stuck in the tents and never make it this far."

An idea jumped into my mind and I said, "I should go out and stop them, tear the tents down, and make it so that people can see the gate as soon as they come out of the darkness?"

The old man reached over and took my arm, "The tents are not the problem. Light cannot be stopped and anyone looking for the source will find it. He then pointed at the gate, "He will make sure of that. Remember, He uses each tent and person for his purposes. You must first tend to your own business."

I took a few steps toward the gate and stared. It rose up into the air and yet was very narrow. About two thirds of the way up the gate there was a slit with a horizontal opening. The gate was so narrow, I wondered if I would fit. As I looked, I realized I would have to lift my arms out sideways and put them into the horizontal bar and then I might make it through. The light itself, was like a fiery wall, yet somehow I knew it was alive. I could feel life blowing from it, or maybe it was more like a current rushing forth. I can't easily say. I stood in awe. This was what I saw in my dreams. I checked to make sure I was clean and prepared and stepped forward.

Then, all of a sudden, I heard my name being called. I raised my head and looked up at the gate and in that moment I was exposed. There was no place to hide, I could run, but now I knew that I was seen and known at the core of my being for what I really was inside.

The motive of my heart was laid bare, every thought was seen. All pretense was stripped away. My very essence lay unveiled.

I was dirty. Not like the dirt that caked on my skin that could be scrubbed off, but like rust, it had eaten into the very fabric of my being and destroyed it. Scenes from my life flashed in my mind like a thief caught on video. I was like an oyster, pried open with no pearl inside. Like a piece of coal, thought to contain diamonds, when crushed, having nothing inside. Like a potters creation pulled out of the furnace, broken into pieces by the flaws exposed in the heat. Exposure was judgment and I was found lacking. I fell to the ground in a heap. Tears flowed and then they also stopped. I had nothing to give and in a horrifying moment I simply admitted and accepted that reality.

As if in response I saw into the light and understood it was not a thing. It was at its center, a person, a relationship. My friend had been right. Darkness was indeed a gift. A tragic gift at that. Just as a little boy might close his eyes on a play ground to think he can hide from his enemies, so with this gift, we could do the same thing to ignorantly protect ourselves from Him.

Yet my friend had been wrong. Yes, reality would pulverize you. If you just saw the exposure, the shame, the guilt, then it was too much for anyone to bear. The weight of the light was so crushing, any hint of deformity, ill-will, selfishness, pride or darkness was immediately exposed by the light. Yet I saw the source of the light and I felt a hand come forth from the light and cover me. No, it held me. No it fixed me. No, no, it hid me. No, it washed me.

In that moment, I knew I was loved. Not because of anything that I did or was. But because of who the light was. I was loved and accepted because He was love and that gave me a freedom I have never known.

My mind rewound to the scenes I had encountered on my way to the gate.

The man trying to fool people by thinking he could sell the light in a box. The seed of desire in people's heart to find the light was so easily perverted by him into a safe sense of ownership without the hassle of getting clean or even finding the gate.

The bath house and the process of getting clean. How easily I had slipped into the false comfort of thinking that if I was clean on the outside, accepted by others and able to fit in among them, then I was clean on the inside.

The tent where they had based all walking in the light on one man's experience with the light. The subtle temptation to create an ideology from somebody else's experiences. Would I be tempted to do it with mine? Those who did not have a relationship with the light would find it so much easier to replace their lack, by adopting someone else's walk with the light. And then, over time, because of this lack, forcing all to follow them in their lack.

Those poor souls who were so distracted by wealth. Thinking they could use their wealth to protect them from the darkness. They could not conceive that a relationship with the light was their only protection. How easily light had opened up ways to see and own new and different things and yet that very awareness became the means of stopping them from going further.

The rides and excitement of the carnival. It may have started with the right motive to get people from the dark into the light. And then it became a means of keeping those in the park from going back into darkness. Yet, how quickly it had become the very thing they had not wanted. It was at best a distraction and stopped so many from going any further and finding the true light.

The man standing in front of the gate wanted to get the glory of being the light. People had gotten so close and yet not been willing to look beyond the man. Their first impression of the truth became their only impression as they were not willing to ask difficult questions and explore deeply to make sure they had found the light.

The supposed safety of the foolish scientists. Thinking their little minds could find all the answers to the light, learn to control it and in essence be the source of the light for themselves and others. Putting complete understanding of the light before submission to what is known of the light was such a subtle blindness.

I stood amazed at how I had made it this far and how easily I could have stayed at any one place and not made it here. I immediately lifted my arms from my side to embrace the light and stepped into the gate. As I stepped in, I also stepped out again at the same moment.

I am incapable of saying what happened. You will just have to trust me that a piece of the light was actually planted into me. No, that is not exactly what I mean. Somehow the light came inside me to live in me. I actually became the light and yet I am not the light. He is the light. I guess it is not a thing that is meant to be described with words, it can only be experienced.

All I can say is that because of this I long to share the light with as many people in the darkness as I can. If only they could know what I have found it would change their life.

Joh 3:19-20 This is the verdict: Light has come into the world, but men loved darkness instead of light because their deeds were evil. Everyone who does evil hates the light, and will not come into the light for fear that his deeds will be exposed.

More Short Stories

The Craftsman

The craftsman examined the rare material held in his worn, tender hands.

Years of agonizing and tedious searching brought him to this moment.

He knew the material was hard to find, yet there could be no substitute, no easy way to do what lay ahead.

The material needed to be tested in order to stand up to the detailed intensity and beauty of his work. He could not settle for anything less, for that would be to cheat himself of his desires and plans. And to cheat himself, selling his gifts for less by using inferior material would be like creating flowers without the smell, a world without colors, or music without any sound. The quality of the material could not be less than his plans and abilities. He would not, He could not allow it, for this was his greatest work.

He heated the oven as hot as he could. Glowing bright orange as only the brightest sunrise could match. Slowly he placed the material in the crucible and closed the door, hoping there would be enough material left over for him to work with.

He didn't know how much would be left. It was as if the material itself decided what it would allow the craftsman to work with.

Seconds dragged into minutes and eternity seemed to wait for the moment. Sweat rolled off the craftsman's forehead as he stood so close to the furnace that the heat seemed to test him as well. Yet, he could not tear himself away from the material at hand for he could see the finished work in his mind in all its dazzling beauty. Time was the only difference between the material and his work, if only it could pass this test.

With a patience and compassion that could not be turned away he waited until the last second, giving every possible chance for anything that could mar his work to be removed.

The time had come as he pulled open the door.

The heat challenged any movement towards its inherent authority.

Yet he stood staring - Eyes aflame.

The Craftsman looked into the material and saw his image reflected back.

Excitement gushed forth.

Tears of joy streamed down his face with a smile that could light the world.

There was enough to do His work.

The craftsman reached down and pulled the man out from the furnace.

The man lifted his eyes and said, "I knew you would come, Lord!"

Magnetic Attraction

A magnet is attracted to iron.

    It is drawn to it, pulled towards it.
    It is influenced by it and focuses on it
    whenever a magnet senses iron is near
    It is affected by it.
    It wants to be a part of it.
    To be joined together.

Imagine a magnet that could produce iron.

    Now that is an amazing thought.
    It could produce the very thing that
attracted it.
    It could determine how strong the pull
was, by creating more or less iron.
    If it created a lot of iron and put it in one
    place, then it would forever be turned
and focused on that place.
    No matter where it was,
    It would always be pulled in that direc-
tion.
    If it created iron and placed it in smaller
amounts, and put it in different places,
    then it would be pulled in different
directions.

Now, imagine that your heart is like that magnet.

You produce the very thing that attracts it.

How do you do this you ask?

By your choices.

Whenever you make a choice, you are investing part of yourself in that choice.

As a result of that choice, your heart will be attracted to whatever you have chosen.

If you make the same choice over and over, the pull will get stronger and stronger on your heart.

If you spread out your choices in a variety of different places, your heart will be spread out in a variety of different attractions.

Remember,

Do not store up for yourselves treasures on earth, where moth and rust destroy, and where thieves break in and steal.

But store up for yourselves treasures in heaven, where moth and rust do not destroy, and where thieves do not break in and steal.

For where your treasure is, there will your heart be also.

The Song

She waited patiently in the little room
knowing that she would be summoned soon.
To be honest she couldn't describe the room,
it had a soft chair by the door which she sat
in and there was a window with a view of the
courtyard. She was so nervous about seeing
him that she could not describe it if she wanted
to.

The last weeks were a blur. She had
been summoned to sing. This was not anything
new as she had been singing since she was a
little girl. And as time went by she was in constant demand. Yet two weeks ago, it seemed
like two years ago, a representative from the
king had come to the door and asked to see her
personally. He would not talk to anyone else.
When the doorman saw the invitation, he realized the representative was for real and let him
in. It was no ordinary invitation. It was sealed
with wax with the king's signet on the back.
She opened it up and stared at it. Real gold
pressed as thin as paper had been used and he
had somehow written a personal invitation on
it. It asked for the pleasure of her presence to

sing for him. That was all it said. She was going to sing for the king.

She had never met him and realized she had been to busy too care. Now she realized, she did care. He was not just any king. He was supposed to be the greatest king of all time. It was said that everyone who knew him, loved him. Excitement began to build from that moment. As she talked with others who had heard about him, her excitement grew. Though before the invitation, in a brief moment of honesty, she confided that her music was "not enough", this had been like new life and reminded her of what it was like as a child, singing before her first audience. Her heart was beating faster and would not slow down.

Two weeks of mind boggling preparation.

What would she wear? Demur? Glamorous? Provocative?

What would she sing? She knew the song had to be something new, never done before. And so with decisions made and remade, a new song written and rehearsed, her day had come.

She had been led to this small room and the man had said that she would be summoned soon.

She went over a few of the lines again in her mind.

Love given, not be to denied.
Yielded to without disguise.

She had never forgotten a line in her life. Yet for the first time it took all her strength to keep the words clear in her mind.

She heard a gentle knock on the door and a voice said, "He is ready, my Lady." She took a deep breath and muttered to herself, "I hope I am".

She opened the door slowly and followed the man down the hall. He arrived at a huge doorway and pulled open the door. No man should have been able to even budge those doors yet it seemed they opened automatically to those summoned by the king. She hesitated for a moment and then moved into the great hall.

She felt Him before she even saw Him. It was like a current of life rushing from Him and yet summoning all things to Him at the same moment. She was drawn toward Him, longing to get just a little bit closer, yet afraid to take another step lest she be found out and pushed away from the wonder of this place.

She heard a voice summoning her forward and inviting her to please come in. She took some feeble attempts at walking and slowly moved forward. The beauty around her took her breath away. Colors almost alive with movement, as if blown by a wind yet she could not feel the wind. Beautiful paintings overflowing, jumping off the walls. Fragrances and smells filled each breath, and created a deeper hunger at the same time. After a few more attempts at what could barely be called steps she entered the main hall and saw Him. After that, nothing else mattered.

All of her preplanned words, her thought-out introduction, her calculated remarks with her most practiced moves, fled. Nothing she had ever been told, or ever had seen prepared her for this. She stood and stared as if struck dumb. Moments passed as the king looked down compassionately on her. When she finally had the courage to look the king in the eyes, her soul burst into flame. Afraid she would be consumed by that which burned within her, she looked away quickly. Feeling completely exposed and vulnerable, fear swept over her. The only movements she had ever learned were those used to entertain and attract men, and to draw attention to herself. She was lost and unsure of what to do.

No audience she had ever sung before had ever prepared her for this. It had all been a distraction at best. She realized, this was what she was made for, this was what she had been looking for all along.

The music started, from where she could not tell, but it was as if it came from the king himself. She stared up toward him and soaked in the beauty of the music. She realized she had never really heard music before, it was as if she had only heard noise compared to this. Like a child's first drawing of a flower compared to being in a field with flowers all about. She reached within herself, summoning all she had, hoping her voice would not fail her now.

She began and poured forth her soul aflame in her song, singing as if she had never sung before.

She continued her song knowing that it was the one thing she had to offer. As she began singing the most difficult part she couldn't believe what she was hearing. The king started to sing with her. He knew her song. Then she caught herself. It wasn't her song, it was His. He had given it to her. How, she did not know, but that He did, there was no question. She sang on, part of her begging to stop and listen to the king singing, another part summoning her to go on as if something would be lost if she didn't. She realized that her voice was not even her own. That all true music and song was His and His alone.

Somehow she realized, again she knew not how, He had given a small part of His voice to her for her to use and express His goodness through. He had given part of Himself to her and she had used it as her own. She stopped singing and fell to the floor sobbing, her heart broken. She had stolen His glory.

Tears flowed as a cleansing agent in purifying her soul. The king sang their song, the words coming to life.

Love given, not be to denied.
Yielded to without disguise.
Who can hide, who can stop
my love I give to you.

She wept and wept as she realized it was His words to her. When she could bear it no more, she looked once more into His eyes and said what she knew was all he ever asked for. "Thank you." He smiled down at her and sang on. She felt Him drawing her to join Him and as He knelt down and offered His hand, she quietly took it and rose to her feet. She began to sing again and she would be the first one to say, it was the first time she had ever truly sung a song.

People always marveled after that day when they heard her sing. Something was different about the way she sang. Her new songs were always filled with thankfulness and tenderness and a new love that led them to believe in the goodness of the King of all Kings.

Raising a Grudge

Grudges are such warm, caring and loyal accomplices. They come in all colors, sizes and shapes. They come to you and accept you just as you are and will always communicate directly how they feel about something.

I am the nurturing type. I like to take care of things and thus help them to grow up and be all they can be. When I am offered an opportunity to care for things, I rarely turn them down. I thought this was a strength of mine but because of it, I have gotten into trouble.

One day, when I was offered the opportunity to care for a Grudge, how could I resist. It seemed too helpless without me.

Grudges are small gifts we receive from others. Those that give them don't see them as gifts, they call them accidents or mistakes and you might hear them say, "I was so tired when I .... that I didn't know what I was doing!", "I didn't mean it that way at all!", "I couldn't help it, they made me do it!", etc., etc.

Why do I call them a gift? Because they are offered to us from others and if we receive them, we can use them to justify things that we secretly want to do. Let me use an example to explain how Grudges are to be raised and their importance. Then I will share how I have gotten into trouble by raising my own Grudge.

A father tells his son that they are going to a ball game together. The son gets excited and can't wait for the day to come. The father has a meeting come up that won't allow him to go. A Grudge is offered to the boy. The first, second or third time the little boy might refuse. He is not ready to take care of it yet. But one time, when the little boy is feeling hurt and unloved, when he wants a reason to be mad at his dad and cover his own pain, he might accept it and try and raise it. Grudges always come weak and helpless and when the little boy received it he immediately started to take care of it. It has to be nurtured and fed in order to survive. Grudges are very hungry and need alot of care. They will eat anything and so the boy started to look for other things the father did in order to feed the Grudge. When the father didn't come to his ball game, that was a good meal for the Grudge. When the father was too busy to play catch with him, another meal taken. With a bigger Grudge the little boy could also justify doing things he knew were wrong but his Grudge protected him. Grudges are fiercely loyal and will never go away on their own. They promise to be a close friend, to comfort their master and stay with them for all time.

My Grudge was offered to me when I was a young girl, 14 years old. My parents were missionaries and they had no place to educate me where they worked so they sent me to a special school for missionary kids in another country. It was an adjustment but I was fitting in. One day the class went to a waterfall for a picnic. The bus arrived at the park near the top of the waterfall. We were going to explore the top and then hike down to the bottom of the waterfall and swim. There was a large pool in front of the waterfall and I immediately jumped out of the bus and pulled my shoes off and ran for the water. I was the first in.

A teacher was running up behind me and yelling but I ignored him. The water was so cool and it was very shallow here. As I entered the water I slipped on the moss covered surface and the current started to pull me towards the falls. I tried to grab something to stop me but it was too smooth. I called for help. The teacher ran quickly into the water and he fell as I had. With his strength he got to me and pushed me to the side where there was less current and I found a hold and pulled myself to the bank. I turned to try and find my teacher and just as I did, I stared in horror as I saw him go over the edge of the falls. He fell to his death.

The pain was more than I could bear. I should have died, not him.

Later, I had to face his wife with their young daughter and although she said it was not my fault and that God was in control, it wasn't OK to me. My young mind agonized, *How could God be in control if He let this happen?*

During this time, I was offered a Grudge. It was small, malnurished and needed my care. My pain was so deep, I immediately accepted it to take my mind off my pain.

After all, I was wrongfully hurt by God's lack of being in control!

I carefully nurtured my new little friend and it comforted me. It quickly grew on me and we became inseparable. He was very hungry however, and I needed to look around in order to continue to feed him. There were other injustices all around me and I fed these to my Grudge. My being dumped at a school and not being with my parents became its food. Stories from others who were hurt or suffering from God's apparent lack of control seemed to come from all around me. A blind man here, poverty there, storms that destroyed thousands of lives. Where was God in all this?

As my Grudge grew, I found I could justify all kinds of wrong behavior. After all, with a strong Grudge to protect me from God, I could not get into trouble. The more wrong I did, however, the more I needed to nurture and care for my Grudge as I needed its protection. He grew and grew until finally one day I realized that I was afraid of him.

Now, no one can comes near me or my Grudge will attack them. I tried to chain him but he easily broke free. He demands my full attention and is jealous of anything else that I do. I even tried to lock him in a room, but he broke out and cannot stand to be alone. I cannot even find enough to feed him and in the back of my mind, I fear he will turn on me.

I know how to take care of a Grudge, that is easy, but I don't know how to get rid of him. The only possible answer I have is that I must kill it. Yet I have given so much of myself to it, I am afraid I will die if it dies.

What do I do?

The Coach

I feel like a failure just when I have reached success. To fail is to succeed and to succeed is to fail. I know that sounds complicated but let me explain.

When I started I didn't have a lot of experience. I had gone through the event myself, so I guess I knew what to expect because of where I had excelled and where I had failed so I took my young students on.

As soon as I got my new trainees I went to work. The early years are slow and you can't push them at all. I just want them to know who I am and to establish a relationship. This is very important.

Slowly their little bodies start to develop and the training begins. First it is just the basics, the old baby steps routine. Just get them to do the basics over and over until it comes naturally.

The bar is set out before them and they have to go under it. It is not much lower than their own height but they can see what their goal is, to get under the bar.

They do it easily. Their young bodies are nimble and they get under it without any problem. You build confidence in them that they can do it. You encourage them often and speak highly of their abilities. Each attempt, no matter how small, is praised. Slowly the standard is raised, which means the bar is lowered. Not by much for you don't want to overwhelm them. They see the lower bar and attempt to get under it. More praise and encouragement as they make the attempt. Either way, if they make it or not, more stretching and strengthening. Years creep by and the bar gets lower and more challenging.

You know in the back of your mind what is coming but you don't accept it. You don't think about it. It is not time yet for the competition. Maybe it will be different.

You push them harder and harder as the date comes nearer. Lower and lower, get stronger and stronger. Push yourself, always maintain control. You can do it.

The day finally comes. All their friends are around. The referee walks onto the floor and sets the bar up. They walk to their place in confidence and look at the height they must get under to pass. They stand in awe. Then it comes, they look to you, their coach and trainer, questions in their eyes. How can they do it? You try and encourage them. Try, just try is all you can say.

They slowly move around and stretch out. They then get down into their, now, very familiar position and inch towards the bar. They strain every muscle in their body as they get closer and closer to the bar. They are lower then they have ever been and still they are too high. They drop another inch, sweating, with slightly cramping muscles. It is now or never. They drop down a little lower and push forward. They run straight into the bar and a loud crash is heard all over the arena as the bar tumbles to the ground.

They strain every muscle in their body as they get closer and closer to the bar. They are lower then they have ever been and still they are too high. They drop another inch, sweating, with slightly cramping muscles. It is now or never. They drop down a little lower and push forward. They run straight into the bar and a loud crash is heard all over the arena as the bar tumbles to the ground.

The student collapses as well. They slowly rise up and make their way off the floor. They embarrassingly look at you and it is then, you teach them what all the training was for. They didn't fail, they succeeded. You reach out and embrace them and encourage them like you never have before. Hopefully, they understand. They can't do it.

• • •

Someone else has done it for them and yet the training was needed.

What does this mean? The coach is a dad who is given children, from God, to raise. He sets the standard about what is acceptable and works hard to train them to be good kids. Hours and hours are spent to train them up in the way they should go. Yet, the training is in one sense, worthless because they will never be able to meet God's standard of moral perfection. They will fail. There will come a time when your son or daughter will give it everything they have and they will not make it under the bar. They will blow it. It will almost be unbearable for the potential shame and yet, it is only then that your son or daughter truly learns that they can't do it. They cannot be perfect as hard as they try. Yet there is hope, for Jesus has found a way for them to make it under the bar, and that they are accepted because of him.

When they fail, only then will they have succeeded to understand that their failure is Christ's success. All the training was to help them see what they could and couldn't do, and what they couldn't do, Jesus did if they would just accept it.

In a sense we train them to deal with their own failure. God will have to show them true success.

Complexity

The father sat reading and heard his little boy's cry before he saw him. A scraggly haired little boy came running into the room with tears dripping off each cheek. He ran to his father and pulled his arm and said, "Quick something is wrong with Chipper, come on". The father reached down and pulled the boy into his arms and they went out to find their puppy.

They made it to the sidewalk and found the brown and white puppy lying silently on the pavement. The father set the little boy down and quickly felt the puppies neck for a pulse. There was none. "He is dead, what happened?" The little boy sobbed loudly in his dad's arms as the pain hit him. With their arms wrapped around each other they both received the comfort they needed. The little boy finally stopped crying and in between sobs and tears explained, "I was Superman, going to save the world, and when I jumped over the wagon, Chipper jumped in front of me. I tried to avoid him but I tripped and fell right on him."

The father nodded his head and said, "Ouch! Accidents happen bud, you couldn't help it and Chipper was just playing with you. He went to Heaven and he felt no pain."

The little boy thought for a minute and said, "Why do people fall and why did Chipper have to die?"

The father sat quietly for a moment and thought to himself. *How can I try and explain gravity and its importance? What about the desire to model heroes and help those in need? What about the complexity of death and its entry into the world?*

The father finally answered, "Those are great questions but they are hard to answer right now. Pain sometimes makes us ask questions that are difficult to answer with words. Let's go bury Chipper and make sure he is taken care of."

The little boy smiled and said "Okay".

He accepted that his father knew and that was enough for him. The father carried the little puppy and they went off to bury their little loved one.

Afterward, the father sat wondering at his boys curiosity and trust. Curiosity to want to know and yet a trust that somehow Dad knew and that was enough for now. The world was safe if Dad knew.

A phone call interrupted his thoughts. He rose from the chair and went over to the phone. The father listened and anyone watching would have seen the tears falling down his cheeks. The words rang in his ears. "He died in an accident".

He set the phone down and dragged himself down the hall with his shoulders drooping and his head hanging low. Not sure of where to go, he found a corner to sit in and wept. Waves of agony unfolded on him. Thoughts began to invade his mind. *How could you allow such pain and injustice God?*

The little boy came back in to ask a question and stood and stared at his Dad. Finally he asked, "Are you still sad about Chipper Dad?"

The father looked up, not realizing his son was there and said, "I am sad about Chipper but I just heard that Uncle died and I am really sad about that." The young boy crawled in his father's lap and asked, "If I have you when I hurt, who do you have when you hurt?"

The question cut to the core of the father as he remembered his earlier thoughts challenging God. He paused for a moment and then said, "God is my father, just like I am your father. I get to go to Him and He comforts me just like I get to comfort you."

"Does he answer your questions for you?" The little boy asked.

The father thought of how God was using his little boy to answer his own questions and responded, "He answers some of my questions but just like I told you earlier, somethings are very difficult for Him to explain right now with words and I trust that for now His knowing is enough for me."

The father broke into tears again and his son joined him. THE FATHER joined them as well and put His arms around them both and it was enough that in their own way each had the answer and ultimately God would work it all out for good.

The Dance

Poems were written, songs sung, old folks talked about it in hushed tones, young people played games about it, but few had seen the dance. Some talked about small teams finding it, but few of these teams ever made it out into the open.

If you talked to ten different people you might get ten different stories about how it worked, or what it was like, but any who saw it, knew immediately what it was. For to see its movement was to see life itself.

Rumor was running around that a dance was going to begin. Some people tried to ignore it, some scoffed and said it was an old wives' tale and just moved on.

Soon, word was out. A dance was beginning. People were walking , some were running, they were headed to the square. Everyone knew that if it truly was the dance, it would be done in the open and the only place that could be, would be on the stage in the square.

A team was on the center stage as the crowd was arriving. Whispers filled the air and moved like a breeze back and forth among those watching. One person in the team reached into his pocket and all noise stopped. Silence covered everything there. They were going to try.

The hand was pulled out of the pocket and a translucent stone was immediately passed in the air. It rose in a slow arch and landed in the hand of one of the younger ones, he clung to it, you could see the weight of it start to pull the young man down.

Just then an old man in the crowd yelled out, "Pass it quick, you can't hold it!" It stirred the young man to action and he managed to pass it back in the air to another before it was too much. The stone was slow moving at first. It moved awkwardly among the group as each member tried to catch its movement and let it flow among them. Soon it was passed higher and quicker and the team spread out.

One team member saw it coming her way and hesitated, the crowd saw her hesitation and gasped, she heard the crowd and reached for the stone but it was past her, somehow, another member had jumped and saved it before it hit the ground and passed it gently above her for her to catch. She was unsure of herself, she quickly grabbed it and pushed it away. The stone dropped like a heavy weight.

It could not be pushed away onto anyone else. It must be caught, and then quickly given, never pushed. Caught and given, caught and given.

One of the team reached out and quickly grabbed the stone before it fell to the ground and sent it back to her as she worked at building her confidence. She reached out and gathered the stone to herself, then just as quickly passed it back into the air for another. She had done it.

The crowd erupted with applause.

The team spread out more now and soon it seemed like the stone was constantly in the air. Its speed increased as the team passed to each other quickly. Movement began as each of the members caught and passed the stone. Each had a unique expression and somehow it all fit together. The stone began to glow with each new expression or movement in the group. It trailed different colors behind it with each new pass. Soon there were rainbows flashing through the air, rising, then falling, flowing among them.

The crowd dared not move. Even the children sat spell bound. They were all afraid any movement would stop the dance.

In one final, last expression, the team seemed to move as one. Brilliant colors, quick movements, each in step.

The stone seemed released from the team. It dashed and flowed among them. A young child from the crowd could bear it no more and yelled, "I see a crown!" Another child yelled, "I see a princess!"

Then it was over, somehow the stone was dropped and it hit the floor with a soft thud.

Everyone stood still. Time stopped. They had seen The Dance. It was more wonderful than any had said.

As people began to slowly drift away a young child walked over and picked up the stone and looked at it carefully. She walked over to her Daddy and asked, "What does it say on here, Daddy?"

Her Daddy reached out and took the stone and read it, "It says 'AUTHORITY,' honey, that is what makes the dance, the dance."

A Buried Treasure

I don't know about you but I like treasures. In fact I used to think I wanted to spend
my life trying to find buried treasures.

I used to dream of finding a Spanish
warship that had sunk offshore in a storm.
Tons of gold bullion lying all over the sea floor.
One day while out swimming, I would discov-
er it.

At other times I would think about
searching an old attic. Opening up a drawer
in an antique dresser and discovering a parch-
ment. Pulling it out and realizing it was a map.
Then following the map to the spot marked X
and digging up a buried treasure.

Still at other times, having an aunt
or distant relative die and being given their
house. Going to the house and finding in the
basement old books and furniture. Discovering
that one book is extremely rare, only ten print-
ed copies left, this one signed by the long dead
author, worth millions. Or how about a stamp
collection of unused stamps that is discovered
and after the dust is blown away, finding in it
a group of stamps that collectors thought were

all gone. Watching it at an auction go for huge amounts of money.

May I say one more fantasy? This is my favorite. Out in the desert or way up in the hills, in the back of some property you own, scouting around and finding an old cave behind a large group of rocks and trees. Squeezing in through a small hole, exploring and finding gold. I first see a few nuggets on the ground and then you trace them to the back wall and realize it is a vein that could go on for miles. I take a handful of these gold nuggets and walk in to town, plunk them down at the bank and now have more friends than I know what to do with.

When these treasures were discovered I would then create this fantasy about how I wanted to spend this untold wealth. Yachts, travel, cars, computers, dare I say girls, I guess you get the picture.

However, now I am not so sure I want to find all these treasures. I have found other treasures and they make my old dreams pale in comparison. I have found these treasures all over. In fact, you may not believe it, but I have actually found them in every city I have been to. I started to travel more and more and every town, village or city I went to, I found places where these treasures were buried. They are not guarded and anyone can go there. Are you interested to know about them?

There are undiscovered works of art and paintings that would compare with Rembrandt or Picasso, a cure for cancer, converting waste to cheap energy technologies, unprinted manuscripts never seen before in poetry, fiction, non-fiction, new songs, unplayed orchestra arrangements, dramas.

If you can dream of it, it is there.

All these gifts stored up and unused. Safely stashed away, unseen by anyone else. Like guarded secrets, kept for the right time that never came. Presents joyfully given, but never opened.

Where are these treasures? I guess I can tell because I can't figure out how to get them. They are in cemeteries or on their way there. Gifts and abilities, treasures placed in people by God, but never used. Hidden away all their life and taken to the grave with them. Buried in unbelief, hidden by insecurity, stomped on by conformity, destroyed by selfishness, entombed in death.

What will you take to the grave with you and who will suffer because of it? What will be buried with you?

2Ki 13:21 Once while some Israelites were burying a man, suddenly they saw a band of raiders; so they threw the man's body into Elisha's tomb. When the body touched Elisha's bones, the man came to life and stood up on his feet.

A Gardener's Care

The Gardener walked out of his house and over to a corner in his yard. He gently bent over. He carefully held the seed in his cupped hand and looked at it. In his mind he saw the seed mature, the image of what it would grow up to look like. It would be beautiful. Careful genetic work had gone into preparing this seed. It was like none other. He would give it special attention.

The soil was spread out among the rocks and full of sand and gravel. It was a harsh land and the Gardener had to trust his skills in order to make anything grow here. He also had to trust the seeds he planted. It was as if they had a will of their own. The land was not friendly and it was only his long suffering and wisdom that allowed there to be any life at all.

He gently pinched the seed between his forefinger and thumb and with his other hand, dug a small hole in the soil for the seed. He reached down with the seed between his fingers and gently placed it in the ground. The seed had to start life in the harsh soil if it had any chance at all to survive later on. He covered it with some soil and watered it.

Then he waited.

Weeks passed and yet on each day the Gardener would go out and check the ground. Nothing.

Finally a small growth broke through. The Gardener smiled and stared with enjoyment. The little seed was growing. It was alive.

More days passed and the Gardener carefully watched over the little life. It would be time for a transplant soon. The soil was so bad that if he misjudged it by a day or two, it might severely damage its life. The timing for each seedling was different and had to be watched over cautiously. It had to have strong enough roots to allow it to grow in the better soil he had scratched together and saved for it in his house, and yet if its roots were too strong, there would be a tearing that would damage the seedling.

The day arrived and the Gardener brought out the pot with the special soil in it that would help the little seedling grow through the winter in the house. He carefully dug around it with his small trowel and loosened the dirt around the plant, but not the dirt in the roots. He carefully lifted the little seedling holding as much dirt to the roots as he could and put it in the soil in the pot.

He moved it into his house with him and would give it special care for the winter. The small seedling had started in the harsh soil and thus could go back out into it next spring and grow to produce fruit. A long winter in soft soil now would not make it too soft to be replanted next year. He looked forward to seeing it full of life and fruit.

This transition was the most difficult process as whenever a seedling was moved, particularly when it was young, it went through shock. It was a battle of wills. The little seeds identity was usually found completely in the soil. When it was taken from the soil and put in a temporary container, it felt cheated, abandoned by the soil it had been born in.

The Gardener talked to the seedling during the winter and gave it special attention. The house was warm and full of life. The Gardener often wondered, *Would the seedling submit to the Gardener knowing what was best? Would it think that the transplant to better soil was a rejection by the harsh soil?*

Some plants were lost because of this shock. It was something the Gardener could do nothing about. The little seedling had to decide where its true life came from. Was it the soil? Or the Gardener?

It was only when the little seedling would respond to the Gardener that he knew it would survive.

One day, long into a harsh winter, the little seedling was set on a window sill to get any light available. As she sat there and stared out into the darkened world outside, she realized how the wind and cold had beaten all living things into hiding. There was no apparent sign of life anywhere. As she sat in the good soil and the comfort of the house she was struck by the Gardeners care for her. With that in mind, the little life humbled herself and responded to the Gardener. She said, "The pain of the transplant is not your fault. I will not blame you anymore. You are only trying to bring good out of a harsh land."

With that the child grew strong and trusted that the Gardener had planted her, wanted her, and would take care of her in whatever soil she found herself in.

She happily responded by bearing fruit.

Death of a Friend

It lay dead. I could hardly believe it. After all those years of training, patience and hard work.

Excuse me, I am getting ahead of myself. You will not understand what I mean unless I give you some history and then maybe you can understand.

As long as I can remember we had been together. In fact we had been inseparable. It was an extension of me.

My earliest memories were of my parents working with me to teach me how to train it. I was taught that I must teach it how to protect and take care of me. First it was trained in simple things, like when and where to go to the bathroom. Though it often demanded and pleaded for its freedom, it was too embarrassing to give it any freedom back then so I kept it with me all the time. Soon it graduated to learning some simple manners. How to keep itself clean and then slowly how to dress itself in such a way as to make itself presentable. I guess it is funny but when you take care of something and teach it such simple things, it becomes a part of you.

The next part was more difficult. I had to teach it how to fit in. This was no ordinary task as it had a wild streak in it that wanted to do its own thing. I worked long hours and I guess you could say, I negotiated with it. I am not proud of what I had to give up, but in the end we sort of compromised and settled into a sense of joining in. It was a constant battle to keep it in line but other trainers seemed to have the same problem so we all gave each other space and worked it out as best we could. The constant encouragement among the trainers was to work harder and train more and that would be the answer.

I must admit, It had an amazing ability to hide itself and mask its true intent. It was like a chameleon that could change its colors depending on the environment it was in. It could charm its way out of anything and could sweet talk a chocolate from a child. It was a very convenient friend when it looked like I was going to get into trouble. There were times I began to think I could actually trust it to behave and it was then, that I learned how quickly it could turn on me and others.

One day I got involved in a relationship. I don't mean just an ordinary relationship, but one where I was head over heels in love. I had never seen anyone more beautiful and I finally realized what I wanted in my life. I wanted an eternity together with that person. Just when I realized this, my lover broke some news to me that, at that moment, shattered my world.

I had a choice to make, it was our relationship together or my life long companion and me alone. I could not have both. I actually begged. We had grown up together, I had trained it and taught it everything I knew. I had taught it manners and how to fit in. It was an extension of me. It was me and I could not let it die, I would die with it.

My lover agreed with me about this challenge but made it very clear that it would not work out for all of us to be together. I had a choice to make and until I made it, I was on my own.

I agonized over this for days. I could train it more. That had always worked in the past, but even as I thought it through I knew it could not work. My love could not be divided, and I had to decide who I loved more. The reality of it hit me like a bolt of lightening. I was tired of trying to train something that couldn't be trained, I wanted love. With this in mind I quickly stood to my feet. I turned to my fleshly nature and killed it.

There it lay, motionless before me. I turned and walked to my lover. A sense of joy rising up within me like I had never known before. We grasped each other and I knew freedom for the first time in my life. My training was done, love was born.

"It" is the Flesh

Eph 2:3-6 All of us also lived among them at one time, gratifying the cravings of our flesh and following its desires and thoughts. Like the rest, we were by nature objects of wrath. But because of his great love for us, God, who is rich in mercy, made us alive with Christ even when we were dead in transgressions—it is by grace you have been saved. And God raised us up with Christ and seated us with him in the heavenly realms in Christ Jesus,

The Enchantment

A Fairy's Tale Adapted from the Work of
C. S. Lewis' Weight of Glory

Fairies come and Fairies go, or so they say I guess. It's just that they never came when I was around. Until tonight that is. I was particularly discouraged with life, wondering why in the world it was made of such pain. My dreams were crashing around me, all I could think about was how things used to be better. Nostalgia was thick in the air. Past experiences with my wife and travel adventures flooded my mind. I thought about my younger years and the tricks we played and the fun it was. My first kiss, oh, my first date. So innocent, so much to learn. As all these memories flooded my mind, I felt more depressed.

In a moment of desperation, I cried out, "I wish....." and I stopped. I didn't even know what to wish for. My mind stuttered and came to a halt. What do you do when you can't even make a wish?

It was then she appeared.

"You called," she replied.

Now I was really confused. "Excuse me?" Was all I could think to say.

She curtsied and said again, "You called me! Whenever anyone makes a wish and doesn't finish it. That is our call. A wish that is not finished leaves a bad mark on our trade you know?"

"Really!" I sputtered. "I didn't know. I guess I didn't finish my wish because I didn't know what to wish. I have run out of wishes. Have you ever heard a sadder tale?" I asked. Daring not to think about what I was talking to.

"That is a sad tale. I must admit." She twinkled and then added, "I can tell you have a wish. I can see it in you."

I laughed out loud. "You have pretty good eyesight. Well, let's see, if you can see it, it must be in me. So, here we go, I wish to understand what has happened to me and why I feel this way!" I hesitated and then added, "I guess what I need is a wise fairy, not just an ordinary fairy."

She curtsied again, and whispered, "I don't know that I've ever met a dumb fairy, though there is rumor they exist. She snapped her fingers and a chair appeared for her to sit in.

"Hey, what about a chair for me?" I exclaimed as she sat down.

"You have a chair beyond you, I won't waste my powers on doing something that doesn't need to be done. Please sit down."

I sat down and she asked, "Tell me the way you feel! I can see wishes but I can't see your feelings."

I settled into my chair and after looking around and realizing that I was alone and no one would ever know about this or believe it. I decided to be completely honest.

I began, "I am feeling out of place. I have lived long enough to have great memories that remind me of the power of life, and yet I am old enough to know that my innermost dreams and secrets lie dying within me and I am afraid they will never be met. I fear that which I long for most will never come true."

"What do you long for most?" She asked.

"I was afraid you would say that. I will only guess and try to put words together to describe something that is never talked about among us. It is like I have within me a few notes to a tune that I have never heard, a taste for a food that I have never eaten, news from country that I have never been to, smells from a flower that I never seen."

"How do you know this?"

I reflected for a while and then said, "I know this because, when I look back at my life I have tasted some deeply wonderful experiences. I have heard wonderful music, tasted exotic food, traveled all over the world and after each of those experiences, I touched something, I heard sounds, I saw pictures that should have made me happy. For a brief moment they did, but then it was gone."

"What do you mean, gone?" She pried deeper.

"I guess I can only use metaphors to describe it. These experiences that I spoke of, they somehow gave the illusion that I belonged, only a moment later to awake and find no such thing. It was like for one brief moment, beauty has smiled, but not to welcome me; her face was turned in my direction, but not to see me. Another way of saying it is that I have not been accepted, welcomed, or taken into the dance. It is like I have overheard a intimate message that was not intended for me."

She asked, "If you went back to those places where the smells, or words or picture were, do you think you would find the fullness there?"

"I have tried to tell myself over and over again that if I could get back there I would be happy. Everyone around me talks as if this were true. Yet, when I am completely honest myself, I have to admit that the tune, taste or picture came through them, it was not in them."

She leaned forward, "You're so honest, most have told me that those experiences, if they could be captured would make them happy."

I open my eyes wide, "You have talked to others about this?"

She chuckled, "I have been around awhile. You humans, you all struggle with this same desire and yet think no one else among you does."

I chuckled with her in embarrassment, "It is kinda silly isn't it."

She almost yelled at me, "No, I didn't say that at all. For a brief moment you are being honest with yourself, I would not call that silly. Courageous maybe, but not silly."

"I think I am just a perfectionist that can't be happy with the simple things. You are probably putting some kind of spell on me even now."

She stood up and began to walk around, "now that is the dilemma you face. Either you were not under an enchantment before tonight and your depression is just causing some temporary problems and what you have seen around you in your life is all the reality there is and I am casting a spell on you which is distorting reality."

At this point the fairy tried to give an evil look but it was completely beyond her to do. Like an innocent child trying to look wicked. She continued, "Or you were under an enchantment before and I am breaking the enchantment with a spell to give you a chance to see reality as it really is or can be."

"What do you mean?" I asked.

"Well, maybe your world is under an evil Sorcerers enchantment that holds you captive. You go through life never able to see past it. Like a fish would never know it is in water because he has never been out of it. Yet, tonight, I break the enchantment with a simple spell and let you see things as they really are."

"But what have I seen?" I pleaded. "I have only said what I have not seen and talked about what I do not know, how can that be spell breaking?"

She hesitated a moment to let my words sink in and then turned to me and said, "Think about it. When you have spent your whole life consumed with only those things which you can see and have only talked about what you do know, these revelations open the door for something far bigger than yourself to enter."

"If I open that door I am afraid of who will enter." The words flooded out before I even had a chance to disguise them.

"Ah Yes, the created before the Creator, finite before the infinite, a subject before the king, a thief before the Judge, a naughty child before the father of all fathers, loveless before the source of love.

"Would it be fair to say that, you are terrified. For you know there is someone that you cannot face and yet the whisperings of his beauty tell you that you cannot live without him."

I took a deep breath. "At a moment like this, I might admit to that."

"Think these thoughts for just a moment and tell me how they feel. You are only passing through this place. You were made for something far richer, deeper, more alive, than anything this world has to offer. Something has happened along the way and now you feel on the outside and the door is closed."

I sat and pondered her words.

"On a more practical note, How can you have desires that no natural happiness will satisfy?"

"OK," I answered, "but being hungry doesn't mean I am going to get to eat. Or having a love for a women does not mean I will get to be with her?"

"Yes that is true," she replied. "But you miss my point, your hunger does not prove that you will get any bread, you may starve to death stranded in a desert. But surely a man's hunger does prove that he comes from a race which repairs its body by eating and inhabits a world where eatable substances exist. In the same way, it would be odd if what you have called 'falling in love' occurred in a sexless world.

"I see your point," I mumbled. "Just because I have a desire for paradise does not mean I will get there, but it may be a pretty good indication that such a place exists and that some men will get there."

"If God made you for his purposes, and even if you didn't care about him, what would be signs of them while living in this world?" She asked.

I chuckled and asked, "Am I asleep and am I hearing one of those TV evangelists in the background?"

She gave me a stern look. "You called me here. Say 'you understand' and I will be gone."

"I was kidding," I said half heartily. "In order for God to get our attention he would almost have to speak through the experiences we have with this world, and yet they could not be all there is or this world be heaven and we would be full."

"So what are your options?" She asked.

"Well, they are pretty painful either way. I can believe that this is just a fairy tale, and you have put a spell on me to talk about and desire things that don't really exist. That this is all there is to life and I might as well get all I can from it. Or, that these experiences are the faint whispering of God telling me of a place that I was made for that is far richer, deeply more beautiful, with things I can only long for here. I must choose which road I will take."

"I guess I have to admit that, I understand." With that she was gone.

I lifted my eyes and wondered if it all was just a fairy's tale or maybe it was the first time in my life I saw things as they really were.

Unbearable Lightness
of Being

We are common people, doing common things, wanting an uncommon experience. You may not understand what I mean, so let me explain myself.

The uncommon experience that we are searching for has to do with our heft, our influence, the capacity to make an impression, the substance of our soul. I guess the best word I can think of to describe it, is 'weight'. I know of no place else to turn but to give you some examples from among us that might help you to understand our struggle.

John is a boxer. He works hard, very hard, to be the best boxer in the world. He trains for hours punching a bag, practicing with others, straining and pushing his body to the limit. He steps into the ring with his opponent who is about the same size and strength as he is and they battle each other, head to head, for 12 rounds. The final bell rings and the decision is made by the judges. John's soul has more weight. He is the winner. It's not really about boxing, it's not about physical weight, for in actual fact John weighs 2 pounds less than his opponent, it's about who is better, and among us it is a common understanding that winners have more weight.

I talked with John later and in a moment of honesty, he whispers to me that though he won, he feels no heavier, but he dare not tell a soul. I saw another old champion who retired a while ago and any weight he gained from his victory is now long gone.

Mark is an actor. He is one of the most popular actors of the day. He has won awards and made millions. His face in on the cover of all our magazines. He has to be careful about where he goes because people will mob him just to touch him. I suppose among us, some think just to touch him will give them significance too. I have heard some say that he has so much weight that he can walk right through people without even noticing them. They are mere ghosts compared to him.

Realistically, I must add that Mark's last film flopped and some say he has lost it. This substance of the soul is very fleeting and often only lasts a very short period of time.

Does this help you to understand us and the challenges we face?

Maybe a few more examples will help.

Mary, wants to be a model. She doesn't eat much and is always looking in a mirror. She is always rubbing her hand down her back side to make sure the curve is still there. She spends hours getting ready and won't do anything that messes up her appearance. She thinks the less she weighs the more weight she has. Does that make sense to you? Cause it sure causes problems with us. Unfortunately we all get old and we know what age will do to her.

Micah is a business man. He owns more money than some small towns. He drives the best car, lives in the biggest house, travels to the best places, and wears the best clothes. You should see how people look at him as he drives by. You can see it in our faces. He is considered a heavy weight. Somehow we believe that each possession or dollar he has goes on the scale with him and when we compare ourselves to him, we come up short, or maybe I should say light.

I could talk about different ones I know from the arts, music or other areas but I think you understand our problem.

I guess among us common folk, we might as well accept the unbearable lightness of being.

The word 'Glory' in the Bible actually means, in part, heavy. You could say God is the heaviest being in the universe. Since he has made us for a relationship with him and wants to live in us. We naturally desire weight for our soul. God is the only one who can give it. It is only as God lives in us that we get the weight we so longingly desire.

What if Evil Were
Like a Strong Wind?

No man knows how bad he is till he has tried
very hard to be good.
C. S. Lewis

The wind had been blowing for so long
and hard that it just seemed natural for everything in the city to be built around it. Architec-
ture, walkways, you name it and the city had
designed it into its way of life. It was like the
current going out over a small gap in the reef,
all the water was rushing to get out of this one
area. Only in this case the water was air and
it was unseen, but its effect was the same. It
rushed, pushed, grabbed and pulled at the city
and anything in its chosen path.

One man always walked with the wind.
In fact he had become so used to it that he
rarely noticed or thought about it. It seemed
easy to go wherever he wanted. He planned
his day to work with it and he tried to take
advantage of it as much as possible. When
asked why he always went with the wind his
comment was, "Wind? Actually it's more like a

breeze, but it just seems the right thing to do. I could go against it if I wanted and it wouldn't be a problem but I just don't want to."

One man always seemed to be going against it. It seemed to always be on his mind as everything he did was affected by it. Even just a short walk had to be thought about in advance. At times he hated it and how it turned everything in its direction, at other times he was thankful for the wind and the strength it built into him. It was a constant struggle and he was not deceived by anyone he knew the strength of the wind and what it could do. But he also knew where he wanted to go and it was not with the wind.

At times when these men would occasionally pass each other. The one walking with the wind would look over at the man walking against it and would see the effects of the wind and would often ask, "Why are you struggling? Life can be so easy. You've got to work with the wind, not against it. I mean anyone could walk against it, but it just works better to flow with it." Sometimes he would even get mad at him for showing how strong the wind was. The other man would just nod his head. He had given up trying to argue about it. It was not a logical issue. Until he wanted more than comfort and his own ease, he had nothing to say that would help him realize how much influence the wind had on them.

The Game Show

You haven't heard about the latest game show? Tell me you're kidding. Tell me you have been on a long trip on a deserted island. Tell me you've been in a coma and have just come out. Just kidding, I guess I better catch you up on the latest news because everyone is talking about it.

People line up for days to get tickets. They can't wait to see what happens. There are actually some people whose goal in life is to wait for tickets and then sit and watch and that is all they do, day after day after day. The tickets are free. If you come to get one they will give it to you. They use huge auditoriums that seat thousands. You do have to be careful because people line up for tickets and then they try and sell them to those who want an easy way to get seats. You can pay thousands of dollars for the best seats if you have the money. The best seats are right up next to the stage. These are for the brave as you actually feel like you are a part of the event and you feel involved. You could see them sweat, feel the turmoil and easily put yourself in their place, yet, you still can't be blamed for anything because you are not playing. The apathy that gives us distance from getting involved may make us uncomfortable at times, but is is a whole lot less than the pain of failing if we try.

I went myself to check it out but I didn't have the best seats. I was in one of the upper levels and I got stuck with some real whiners. I mean you should have heard them. Once they settled into their safe little seats they started up. Their view wasn't good enough. The lighting was bad. They were cold and it was too far to walk to the restroom. Finally, I got so mad I told them to be quiet. I then said something I probably shouldn't have said. I told them if they didn't like where they were why didn't they just play the game? That shut them up.

I decided I would try my luck again and got some better seats. I sat there and listened and got just as mad. I mean everyone had an opinion about what the person should do, what the best strategy was, how to react, when to give or get, dodge or attack, move or sit still, I mean everyone around me had an idea that they were sure would work. I finally told them the same as I told the others and they immediately were silenced as well.

You see, the amazing part is that we don't have to be a spectator. If you want, you can play the game show and be involved. It is easy to do and they need more people then they can get. I heard someone explain the difference between watching and actually getting involved as the difference between watching a romantic film and actually being in love. Someone else explained it as the difference between looking at someone elses family pictures and growing up in the family yourself. A sense of ownership and joy from actually taking a chance and getting involved. Most of us have decided to get involved, but it is always, another day, another time, just not right now.

It is a shame because they could open up in new places all over if they just had more people involved. I thought about it myself but it is so much easier just to watch. I mean it is one thing to watch someone win or take a chance and to risk it all, I really enjoy that, but to think about me doing that personally, ugh, it gives me the shivers just to think about. What would happen if I lost. How could I face others who would tell me a thousand times what I should have done. No thanks, I think I will find a nice safe seat and just watch.

What is the game show? What is the event? It's simple. It's called 'Life.'

About the Author

Matt Rawlins works internationally with the University of the Nations as a teacher, trainer and consultant dealing with leadership and organizational issues.

With a Ph. D. in Philosophy (specifically in leadership and communication), Matt has a heart to see people understand who they are and specifically, to help leaders communicate about difficult issues in times of change.

The author of 9 books, Matt is a gifted writer and communicator.

After living in Asia for ten years, he now resides with his wife Celia and son Joshua in Kailua-Kona, Hawaii.

You can contact him at:
        mrawlins@hawaii.rr.com

www.ingramcontent.com/pod-product-compliance
Lightning Source LLC
Chambersburg PA
CBHW031845170626
46807CB00004B/1628